THE TALE OF NAUGHTY MAL
and other donkey stories

THE TALE OF NAUGHTY MAL
and other donkey stories

Dr Elisabeth D Svendsen MBE

Illustrations by Eve Bygrave

Whittet Books

First published 1994

The Tale of Naughty Mal © 1994 by Dr Elisabeth D Svendsen MBE
More Adventures of Eeyore © Published by the Donkey Sanctuary 1978
Eeyore Meets a Giant! © Published by the Donkey Sanctuary 1987
The Story of Jacko – the Hurricane Donkey © Elisabeth D Svendsen 1982
The Champion Donkeys © Published by the Donkey Sanctuary 1989

This edition published 1994

Whittet Books Ltd, 18 Anley Road, London W14 0BY

The Donkey Sanctuary is at Sidmouth, Devon EX10 0NU. Tel no 0395 578222

Text and cover design by Richard Kelly
Cover illustration of Mal with Ellen by Eve Bygrave

A catalogue record for this book is available from the British Library

ISBN 1 873580 14 2

To my grandchildren
Mark, Dawn, Kate, Simon and Sam

Contents

The Tale of Naughty Mal
11

Eeyore Meets a Giant!
25

More Adventures of Eeyore
37

The Story of Jacko
the Hurricane Donkey
53

The Champion Donkeys
69

Sam

Mal

Jacko

Dobby

Eeyore

Foreword

This is a book about my favourite animal, the donkey. I have always loved donkeys, and since I was a little girl of five I have been entranced by their gentle nature, beautiful eyes and their kindness, which I have witnessed on my travels even when they are being ill-treated!

I have been so lucky in that, for the last twenty-five years, I have been able to look after them all the time — I am "Mother" to over 6,000 donkeys in our Sanctuary here in England, and "Mama Punda" (Swahili for "Mother of the Donkeys") to donkeys in Africa and throughout the world!

Eeyore used to be our naughtiest donkey, but we lost him a little while ago. He died very suddenly and we were all very sad. However, we now have another donkey called Mal, who seems *just* as naughty, and no doubt he will have many adventures at our lovely Sanctuary here in Devon.

As well as looking after donkeys that get into trouble in Great Britain and keeping them for life, through our overseas charity, The International Donkey Protection Trust, we look after donkeys all around the world. Even on holiday I always look after donkeys, and I met Jacko and his family while on holiday in St Lucia.

Donkeys abroad work very, very hard carrying goods, pulling carts and ploughing the land. We help to make their life easier, and find ways to help them, which is why "The Champion Donkeys" story is so important.

I do hope you enjoy these stories and the lovely pictures that go with them.

If you want to help donkeys, please write to us at the Donkey Sanctuary, Sidmouth, Devon EX10 0NU. We promise to write back!

Mother

THE TALE OF NAUGHTY MAL

Mal's story begins when his mother Ellen was rescued from working on a beach in the north of England. Poor Ellen: after working hard all day, giving ride after ride without a rest or a drink of water, she had to go back with all her friends to a dark and dirty stable where she was given hardly anything to eat.

Tired and hungry, Ellen would desperately try to find a little hay or straw she could eat from the dirty smelly bedding, as she knew she must try to eat plenty, for soon she would have a baby to look after. The stable was very, very full, as she lived with thirty-four other donkeys. As the summer went on Ellen grew more and more exhausted, and her best friend, Sara, became so thin she could hardly stand up.

One day, something happened. Ellen had just come back from a

Sara and Ellen lying on the beach.

horrible ride. The boy on her back was far too big, and he had kicked and shouted at her, and had frightened her so much that she had galloped back to the other donkeys, panting and sweating and feeling ill.

To Ellen's surprise, the owner was shouting loudly — not at the other donkeys as he usually did, but at a man who was stroking and loving Sara, and, taking off her heavy saddle, dropping it on the beach!

All the donkeys stood watching, glad of the few minutes' rest. Sara, the weight taken off her back, had quietly sunk to the ground, and was stretched out, too tired to even lift her head. Suddenly the man moved to Ellen, and the cruelly tight girth around her swollen stomach was loosened, the saddle lifted, and she too was able to sink to her knees.

The donkeys watched as the two men argued and then, to the donkeys' horror, the kind man moved off, but he turned back and shouted, "I will be back."

The owner quickly started taking rides again, but he left Sara and Ellen lying on the sand. They both watched and waited, and hoped the kind man would come back.

It must have been half an hour later when Ellen realized she had been sleeping, because a whole group of men were now arguing with the owner, including a policeman, who was very cross. "Disgraceful — disgusting — these poor donkeys should not be working," he was saying. The kind man from the Donkey Sanctuary was on his knees by Sara. "We have two lorries on the way," he said, "we want to take them all to our Sanctuary in Devon." Ellen did not know what a Sanctuary was, but she knew it must be better than working on the beach, and she really liked the kind man who was stroking Sara.

Very soon Ellen heard the noise of a big lorry, and she and Sara were gently helped aboard. They were just glad to rest rather than struggle up and down the beach.

Ellen must have gone to sleep again, because when she woke up the back of the lorry was open, and, with Sara and her friends, she looked out at a sea of friendly faces and beautiful green fields. Gentle hands were helping all the tired donkeys off the lorry, and Ellen could hear the voice of a lady everyone was calling "Mother" talking to them all gently. "Come along, donkeys, you are all safe now and will never have to work again. We've got big warm stables ready with lots of straw to lie on, a lovely hot bran mash and plenty of hay to eat."

One by one they were petted and loved as they came off the lorry. Sara and Ellen were the last, as they were both lying down. Everyone went very quiet as they walked into the lorry to help them to their feet — Sara was too weak and thin to manage on her own, and Ellen was nearly ready to have her baby.

"How could they?" asked Mother quietly, and Ellen and Sara felt

The saddle was lifted and Ellen too was able to sink to her knees.

her tears falling on their muzzles, as, with help from Mother and all her staff, the donkeys were lifted up and helped to warm stables. It was like a dream come true for them, and, as Mother and her staff left, after making them comfortable, the little donkeys just could not believe their good fortune as they rested under the heat of an infrared light. Then they began to eat their first beautiful warm meal in years!

Over the next few weeks the donkeys began to feel better; kind vets came, and, although they were not too pleased to have injections, all the donkeys knew it was to help them. It was lovely to have their feet trimmed and to be able to look forward to a gallop in the green fields which they could see from the stable doors!

Ellen and Sara stayed together in the same stable, as Mother felt

they both needed extra care. One night Ellen began to get a very bad tummy ache. "Quick, Sara," she said, "bray for Mother," and Sara brayed and brayed until Mother came. By this time, Ellen was lying down, and right next to her was the dearest little foal that Mother had ever seen! He was light brown, with a pale brown muzzle and extremely long legs. "Why, you clever girl," said Mother, stroking Ellen. "What a dear little foal! Thank you, Sara, for calling me."

Within minutes the little foal was tottering about on his long, spindly legs, and, as Ellen stood up, he began pushing her and trying to find the milk he knew should be there somewhere. First he tried under her front legs, but there was nothing there. Then Mother gently helped him to Ellen's udder which was dripping with milk. He clamped his little lips around the teat and began to suck noisily, with Mother holding him.

Suddenly he felt he could manage on his own and, with his long

Ellen and foal.

16

back legs, he tried to give Mother a kick! Of course he lost his balance, and fell in a spindly heap on the floor! Mother was laughing so much she could scarcely help to pick him up. "You naughty little donkey," she said. "You're just as bad as Eeyore was!" Ellen looked at her young son, and agreed!

Mother had a very special helper called Mal, and so when Ellen's baby was born he was named after her.

At first Mal was not very well. The fact that his mother had been so very badly treated before he was born had made him rather weak, and he developed a bad cough. But, even if it was raining, he was so curious that he couldn't bear to stay in the stable if he heard anyone outside. He just would not stay in unless the door was tightly shut. As his cough grew worse, Mother and the vets decided he had better go into the Donkey Hospital where he could *not* get out into the rain, and the vets and nurses could be with him all the time. Ellen did not

He wanted to help everybody *when they were cleaning out.*

mind at all — it was lovely and warm and she had all the food she could eat and a lovely bed to lie on. The nurses had quite a job with Mal. He wanted to help *everybody* when they were cleaning out the stable. He did enjoy playing with the wheelbarrow and the brushes! As for injections — he soon noticed when the vet came in with a syringe, and would dodge from corner to corner! After a few weeks of special care his cough disappeared, and Mal and Ellen were able to return to their own stable.

With good food and proper care, Ellen and Mal got strong again, and the little donkey grew and grew. But Mother had been right! Mal was a naughty little donkey. One of the best games he liked to play with his mother was to nip her back legs and then run away. As he grew bigger he used to run straight at Ellen, jump up and land with his long front legs right up over her shoulder! Poor Ellen, she

had quite a job with him, but not such a difficult job as Colette, the groom, whose job it was to look after Mal.

His favourite trick was to untie Colette's shoe laces, hold them in his teeth and refuse to let go! He also loved the toggles on her coat, which he would grasp with his little teeth and, looking straight into Colette's eyes, he would pull madly; nothing would make him stop until he was ready to let go.

One day Colette had to call John, the farm manager, to show him the fences and the stable door that Mal had been chewing — there was hardly any wood left! Poor John, whilst he was looking at the fence, Mal crept up behind him and pushed him against the rail! When John managed to free himself and walked away across the field, Mal chased after him at a gallop, flicking his little heels as he passed, and kicked John on his hand. He was naughty!

Of course Mal had many visitors, who loved to see the three donkeys together. "Aren't they sweet," they would say, leaning over the fence. But woe betide the visitors if they were holding anything in their hands, because Mal loved nothing more than a gallop with someone's camera dangling from his mouth!

The three donkeys lived in their own special area which had two large airy stables, a run-out yard and a lovely grassy paddock. They received a great deal of attention from everyone who passed by.

When their little yard was used to teach

His favourite trick.

19

some new donkey owners how to handle their donkeys, Mal did not miss the chance to be naughty. The teacher tied Ellen up at one end of the paddock, with Mal, of course, at his mother's side, whilst the teacher demonstrated how to pick out a hoof correctly. In the middle of the lesson everything went terribly wrong! Mal had untied Ellen's rope and now, holding it in his teeth, he charged through, dragging his mother with him.

As Mal grew bigger, Mother sometimes let the three donkeys go into the main yard where some of the elderly donkeys lived. These "granny" donkeys — some nearly fifty years old — enjoyed living in the yard, as they could meet the visitors there and have lots of love and attention.

One of these donkeys was called Mary. She was very adventurous, but no-one knew quite how many tricks she could do. One Saturday morning, Mary set up Mal's first *really* naughty trick!

Mother had finished work for the day and with June, who lived with her, had gone shopping. Mother's house is right opposite the Sanctuary and she had left the drive gates open so that she could drive straight in on her return.

The yard had a very large, heavy, green gate which was fastened by a heavy bolt. It was, Mother had said, "donkey proof". But that was before Mary got her teeth round the bolt! How she did it no-one knew, but she managed to open the gate, and she went through to explore, closely followed by her mother, Sniffy, and friend, Minnie, who always stayed together. Ellen never noticed the open

Mary opening the gate.

gate, but guess who did? Mal, of course! The naughty little donkey trotted after the others.

Mother just could not believe her eyes when she came back and turned her car into the drive! There, pruning her roses and munching the lawn, were three donkeys, dressed smartly in their waterproof coats, and thoroughly enjoying themselves! June ran over to the Sanctuary for help, and Ron, Glynis and Kate rushed with her to lead the donkeys back to the yard. Mother and June were amazed that they had managed to open the gate and, having made quite sure that Mary and her friends were safely shut in again, they went back to have lunch. Mother had noticed Ellen in her stable, and felt sure that Mal

Mal pulling his mother.

21

Donkeys eating roses on Mother's lawn.

would be with her. Nobody even *thought* that the naughty little donkey would have left his mother and followed the others.

Mal did not fancy eating the roses, they had nasty thorns. Enjoying being out on his own, he had trotted around to the back of Mother's house to see what was there. To his great delight he found a pond. He had never been able to paddle in water before, and he couldn't wait to try it! He gingerly stepped into the water and then, realizing it was not deep, began splashing about and, having examined the water lilies floating on the surface, delicately picked the flowers off with his sharp little teeth!

Mal really was enjoying himself. When he grew tired of the water, he trotted across the lawn, leaving little hoof prints in the soft grass, and found Mother's flower beds. Mother had spent years planting flowers, and in the middle of the bed she had planted a beautiful apple tree. Mal decided he didn't like pansies, he didn't like roses, but he did like the taste of the apple tree leaves! He reached up to the very top of the tree for the most delicious new shoots.

Mother and June were quietly enjoying their lunch when they happened to glance through the window. "Oh my goodness," they both shouted at once, and they rushed out of the door into the back garden. Mother did not have to look at the donkey's collar — she knew who it was! "Mal, you really *are* naughty. Just wait until you get back to your mother. She will be so worried that you are missing — and look at my apple tree — and why are you so dirty and wet?" Then Mother saw the muddy pond and the water lilies with all the flowers missing and the hoof prints in the lawn.

By now Mal was beginning to feel just a little bit sad. He could see he had hurt Mother and had never, ever, heard her sounding cross before. He hung his head down, and felt very, very sorry he had been so naughty.

Mal eating the apple tree.

Mal having a cuddle.

But of course Mother was *not* cross; it was just that she was so worried to think of all the trouble Mal *could* have got into. Perhaps he could have drowned in the pond, or eaten some poisonous plants or been run over if he had strayed out onto the road!

Suddenly, Mal felt Mother's arms around his neck and felt a big cuddle, and as he looked up, he saw June laughing as she reached out to stroke his nose. He found himself being led gently back to his stable.

You should have heard the braying as he returned! The "eeyores" rang round the yard as everyone joined Ellen and Sara, who by now had missed Mal and were really worried. As Mother and June put him into the stable, Ellen gave him a hard nip on his front leg, just to let him know how cross she was with him.

Mother leant over the door and said, "Oh, Mal, I do believe you really are the naughtiest donkey in the Sanctuary." June, Ellen, Sara and all the donkeys in the yard agreed!

I wonder what he will get up to next — don't you?

EEYORE MEETS A GIANT!

Eyore was well known as the naughtiest donkey in the Sanctuary. His mother, Smartie, had arrived in the most terrible state — so thin that two people could carry her and covered in sores.

Mother had to sit up with her all night, spooning glucose and water into her mouth until she was strong enough to start eating for herself. Her feet had not been looked after, and had grown longer and longer until she could not even stand up properly. The man who used to own her had sent her to a market to be sold when she was too ill to give rides on the beach any more. A kind lady bought her and sent her to the Sanctuary.

The Donkey Sanctuary is in Devon, and looks after any donkey that gets into trouble. To many donkeys, after years of hard work and bad treatment, it is heaven to find lovely big green fields to gallop in, warm airy stables to sleep in and all the favourite food they need! All this plus love and attention should keep any little donkey happy — except perhaps Eeyore!!

Shortly after she arrived, Mother realized that Smartie was in foal,

Poor sick Smartie.

26

and due to have her baby very soon. The minute he was born Mother cuddled Smartie and said, "You clever girl! What shall we call him?" Smartie threw up her head and gave a great bray. "Eeyore" she said, so the baby was called Eeyore. From the moment he was born, he led everybody a dance.

Poor Smartie would stand by the fence, and Eeyore would dodge underneath it and gallop around just out of her reach, eating Mother's best roses.

He pinched the fire buckets and ran round the field with them.

He pinched the bobble cap from a little boy's head, and, even worse, he pinched the handbag of a headmistress who was leaning over the fence telling her class of children how sweet little donkeys were!

Baby Eeyore with the Headmistress's handbag.

Eeyore grew up happily with his firm friends, Ruff, Pancho and Frosty, and despite many adventures and being terribly naughty, Mother and all the donkeys loved him.

Every day the Sanctuary lorry went out to collect donkeys in trouble, and on this particular Tuesday, Perry, the driver, had to go to Derbyshire where he had six donkeys and one mule to collect and bring to safety. Now a mule has a horse for a mother, and a donkey for a father. Mules are usually bigger than donkeys, but have some parts like a horse, some like a donkey. Sometimes the mother is a donkey, and the father a horse, and, although they are still mules, these animals are known as hinnies.

Perry collected his first two little donkeys called Bill and Ben, then went to collect Jubilee, the mule. He just could not believe his eyes. She was enormous!

The man who had bred her had grown to love mules in the army. The soldiers used them to carry heavy goods. They were very strong, but rather obstinate. Every time they came to a river, they would refuse to cross until a little female donkey called a "bell" donkey

He collected Bill and Ben.

went across first. Then they would all follow her, her little bell ringing out to tell them it was safe!

Jubilee's owner decided to breed the biggest mule in England. He chose the mother carefully, a sister of a famous racehorse called "Rubstic" who had won the Grand National. That's the race with the enormous fences the horses have to jump. For the father, he chose a very special donkey, very, very big with long hair, from France — called a Poitou. His name was Eclair.

Jubilee was born in 1977, the Queen's Jubilee year and that is how she got her name.

Unfortunately, her owner became ill, and Jubilee was sent to a horse stable to be trained to pull a cart, but Jubilee did not like that. One day she would be very, very good, but the next day, she would gallop away and go so fast that the cart would turn right over and everybody be thrown out. She was so big and strong that no-one could be sure what she would do next, and she really became rather naughty. One day her owner decided that she could not manage her any more, and decided that she should go to the Donkey Sanctuary.

When Perry arrived, he and Jubilee stood looking at each other! Perry had collected almost all the 3,000 donkeys to come into the Sanctuary, but *never* one like this! He carefully measured her, and then went back to the lorry and measured that! She would just fit in, but he would have to take her back to the Sanctuary with Bill and Ben. There was no room for any more! He rang Mother, who could hardly believe her ears, and she rushed off to find John, the vet, so that they could find a big enough stable.

It was a long way home, and Jubilee felt very sad to be leaving Derbyshire. She did not know where she was going and she did not

Perry carefully measured her, and then measured the lorry.

Donkeys need big ears and big voices.

particularly like the two little donkeys who kept staring up at her from their partition in the front of the lorry. A big tear ran down her cheek as she wondered what on earth would happen to her next!

It was dark when the lorry arrived, and Mother and John stood watching with the big yard lights on as Perry opened the ramp! "My goodness — I don't believe it!" said Mother, but John, who had looked after horses before he had joined the Sanctuary, seemed really pleased to welcome the latest of his charges.

If Mother and John were surprised, what do you think the donkeys thought! They always welcome new arrivals with a bray, and in donkey language try to reassure them that they are going to have a lovely time, but for once, they, too, were shocked into silence!

John led Jubilee into the biggest stable the Sanctuary had. It had plenty of headroom, and Jubilee could look out over the door and see the donkeys.

Bill and Ben were led into the airy barn where the new arrivals went. They quickly told the donkeys there about the new arrival! How fast the news spread! Donkeys have been given big voices to shout with, and big ears to listen with, as in the early days, the horses took the meadows rich in grass, and pushed the donkeys up the hills and mountains. So they needed big ears and voices, and on that night the brays spread round the valleys.

Eeyore was asleep in his shelter at the other end of the Sanctuary. He woke up when he first heard the braying, and he and his friends Ruff, Pancho and Frosty decided they just *had* to see for themselves.

"I'll check the gates," said naughty Eeyore, "I've been good so long they may have forgotten to put the chain on." Although the chain was on, the padlock was not properly shut. Eeyore twisted his neck round, and got his little teeth round the hasp. He pulled and pulled, and suddenly the padlock fell to the ground. The four friends pushed on the gate together, but it would not move.

"Come on, all together!" brayed Eeyore ."One, two, three, *push*!" and they all pushed and the gate opened — so suddenly that Frosty fell right on top of Eeyore! When they had got back on their hooves, Eeyore led the way importantly along the lane, and down the track to the isolation boxes.

"Where is this thing?" he asked Bridget, one of the oldest

Frosty fell right on top of Eeyore.

31

The most enormous "donkey" he had ever seen.

donkeys, who had a special knitted blanket on her back, and a warm infra-red light in her stable.

"Over there, Eeyore, in stable 11," she said.

Eeyore went, and stared into the stable and then *suddenly* he saw the most enormous donkey he had ever seen.

Jubilee looked down at him. She was really feeling even more miserable. Despite the warm box and the lovely hay, she was missing her horse friends and she was beginning to think she didn't like donkeys.

"Go away, you nasty little donkey," she said, "leave me alone. I don't want to talk to anyone," and she turned her back on Eeyore.

"Nasty little donkey?" said Eeyore "Me? I'm the most important donkey in the Sanctuary, so you'd jolly well better be polite to me!"

Jubilee had had enough. "You cheeky young donkey," she said, "I'll teach you a lesson," and she ran at the door meaning to stick her head out and give Eeyore a shock, but, oh dear! the door had been built for donkeys, not the largest mule in England! With a horrible rending crash, the whole door broke, and Jubilee plunged into the yard, with the frame round her shoulders and broken wood everywhere!

Eeyore, Frosty, Pancho and Ruff were terrified — they galloped desperately up the track, hearing Jubilee's hooves pounding behind them.

"Quicker! Quicker! She's catching us!" brayed Frosty.

But Eeyore was stopping. He could no longer hear Jubilee's hooves.

Eeyore looked around. There was Jubilee, standing on the track. The frame was round her

Jubilee coming through the door.

Galloping desperately up the track.

neck and she was trembling from head to foot — Eeyore looked closer, surely that wasn't … but it was. Great tears were running down Jubilee's beautiful muzzle and splashing onto the ground.

Eeyore hesitated a moment, and then slowly walked towards her. Silently they looked at each other, and a strange feeling came over both of them.

"Frosty, Pancho, Ruff, come here please," said Eeyore quietly. "Frosty, you push the frame at that side. Pancho, you go to the other side, and Ruff and I will pull from the front. Put your head down, Jubilee."

The four little donkeys pushed and pulled until at last Jubilee put her head back up, the frame no longer round her shoulders.

"Thank you, Eeyore," she said, "I feel better now."

For a few moments nobody moved. Then Eeyore made a big decision.

"We will stay with you tonight, Jubilee," he said. "Come back with us to our stable. Mother is sure to find you in the morning."

And Eeyore, rather proudly, led the big mule and the three little donkeys back up the lane and into their own home. All the little donkeys waited outside until Jubilee had found a nice place to lie down in, and then, one by one, they carefully stepped around her, until they found an empty space. Eeyore lay right next to Jubilee, and as they dropped off to sleep Eeyore's head was close to Jubilee's.

What a morning that was in the Sanctuary! There was panic when John, going to check the new arrivals, found the box empty and no Jubilee! Everyone rushed off to find her, and Mother was so upset that it was some time before she began to think clearly but, suddenly, she stopped searching the fields and shouted, "I bet it's Eeyore!"

Everyone stopped looking, and all the staff, with Mother in the lead, went to Eeyore's field.

All the little donkeys waited outside.

Eeyore and Jubilee.

First they found the gate open. "Oh dear, I knew it would be something to do with Eeyore," wailed Mother, and then she saw John beckoning from the stable.

They all looked in. The friends were still fast asleep, tired out after their adventures, but Eeyore lifted his head and looked at Mother.

"Oh, Eeyore, I should be so cross with you," she said. "But thank you for looking after Jubilee. You're not *always* the naughtiest donkey!" and she ran in and gave them all a big, big cuddle.

MORE ADVENTURES OF EEYORE

Eeyore with a mouthful of hay, trying to unbolt the door.

Do you ever get the feeling that whatever you do, nothing goes right? That was just how Eeyore was feeling one bright, cold, sunny morning.

The day had started just as every other morning he had known in the Sanctuary, with the welcome noise of buckets rattling in the feedhouse, and the cheerful chatter of men greeting each stable of donkeys in the intensive care unit as the breakfast came around.

"Come on, Lucky Lady, come on Pop, you have got a really special bran mash this morning!" he heard John say next door, and then it was their turn. With Ruff, Frosty and Pancho, he eagerly

Eeyore, Frosty, Ruff and Pancho awaiting breakfast.

awaited the delicious donkey nuts that he and his friends had for breakfast. They were not the sort of nuts you and I would think of; these were made of bran, crushed oats, and chopped dried grass, and to Eeyore and his friends they were beautiful. He loved the clatter and rattling noise as they were tipped into his food tray. Some of the other very old and sick donkeys in the intensive care unit had to be coaxed to eat their breakfast, and some had almost worn their teeth completely away, and had to eat soft bran mashes with black treacle in it, but not in Eeyore's stable. They never needed to be told to eat it all up.

Before they had finished, their hay rack had been filled up with fresh sweet hay, and Eeyore pulled out a large mouthful, before walking over, and leaning out of the door as far as he could.

"Bother!" he thought.

"It really is tightly bolted. I *do* wish they would forget again sometimes." But of course since his last escape, everyone was always especially careful about *his* door.

He watched as all the old and recovering donkeys were let out from the stables, and walked or trotted across the yard and into the special field where they spent the day. It was a gentle sloping meadow, and there was a shallow pond in one corner. Eeyore watched carefully; he had had a naughty idea the day before as he had watched Gertrude quietly dozing in her favourite place right at the very edge of the water, under the trees.

He noticed that Mother had put a rug on Gertrude and many of the older donkeys, as it really was quite chilly, despite the sun.

At last it was their turn to go out. No gentle walking for Eeyore. As soon as the door was opened, he trotted across the yard with his three friends, and then went for a good gallop around the edge of the field. After a few moments, Eeyore slowed down, and then sneaked a glance at the pond. Yes, there was Gertrude, just dozing off and right by the edge!

Eeyore left the others, and wandered nearer and then — that naughty little donkey accidentally (or on purpose) bumped into poor old Gertrude as he passed her!

Gertrude did not really realize what had happened until she felt the cold water over her fetlocks. With a startled cry she brayed for help.

Herb, who groomed the donkeys every day, and kept their eyelids nice and moist with baby oil, had seen exactly what had happened.

"You young monkey!" he called, "I may have been grooming Lucky Lady, but I saw what you did, and you are in big trouble now."

Then he went to tell Mother.

By the time she arrived, Eeyore was looking very innocent, quietly grazing with his friends. Mother came straight over to him, a halter in her hand. This time, Eeyore realized that he had gone too far.

"You really are a very naughty little donkey, Eeyore," she said. "Poor Gertrude! How could you be so unkind to her? You were very lucky to be born in the Sanctuary and nothing really nasty has ever

Gertrude stood, head drooping, legs dripping.

Eeyore was shut in alone.

happened to you, but Gertrude has had a very unhappy life and she needs all the kindness and help that we can give her now."

Eeyore tried to look sorry, but he kept thinking of the pond, and how funny Gertrude had looked!

Mother realized that he was not really sorry at all and she slipped the halter over his head. Before he realized what was happening, he was being led back to his stable alone.

"There," said Mother, closing the door firmly. "Perhaps on your own you will have time to think about things, and decide how you can *help* others in the future," and she went away.

Poor Eeyore! He could not remember ever having been so alone in

*There he was on
the little lane that
led to Salcombe Regis.*

his life. He lay down, to think over what Mother had said. He felt very sad and sorry for himself, and closed his eyes and tried to imagine his friends were with him. Eeyore fell into a deep, deep sleep …

It seemed as if no time had passed at all, when he lifted up his head to find the door wide open! He stood up, and moved to the door quietly and looked out.

It was amazing … there was no-one in the yard. He walked out, and turned up onto the drive. Gracious, he just could not believe his luck … the main Sanctuary gates were open! He broke into a trot and there he was, on the little lane that led to Salcombe Regis.

He had always wanted to go down to the village … Pedro had been twice and had been full of stories about

how he had panniers on his back, and collected money at the Village
Fete. At a brisk trot he set off, not even stopping to think how
worried everyone would be when they found his stable empty.

It was further to the village than he had thought, but soon he was
trotting down a little lane with houses on either side.

"My goodness," he thought, looking at some beautiful flowers in
one of the gardens, "those do look delicious!" And he leant over the
wall and tried a mouthful. He was not quite sure whether he liked
them or not, and before he had decided, he saw the most prickly
stemmed plants he had ever seen. Now donkeys love thistles and
prickles, and Eeyore did not know that Mr Green had spent many
years growing his prize roses, so he stretched his neck as far as he
could over the wall and slowly munched Mr Green's very best
rosebuds!

Despite being prickly, they were nice and juicy, and he ate all he

Eeyore eating Mr Green's roses.

44

A large gate, it was the Vicarage.

could reach before he left the garden, looking a little bare, and went
on down the road.

Facing him at the bottom of the hill was a large green gate ... it
had a long word on it. It said "VICARAGE" but of course, Eeyore
could not read it.

He gave the door a push and, rather to his surprise, it opened and
he stood in a little courtyard.

A small path ran around the side of the house, so Eeyore decided
to explore it. He arrived on a lovely lawn and, quickly going past the
rose bushes, he arrived at the Vicar's vegetable garden.

Oh dear. The Vicar had spent many back-breaking afternoons
tending his vegetables, and the carrots were just ready for pulling.

Oh what a naughty Eeyore ... he just could not resist them! Once
he had tasted one, he worked his way steadily up the row, pulling out
the juicy young carrots, munching them with an expression of bliss
on his face. He got to the end of the row, and turned around to look

45

for something else. Aha, a row of fresh green lettuces! He was just about to start into them, when he heard a strange, loud noise.

DING-DONG … DING-DONG …

Eeyore decided to investigate. He quietly went down the Vicarage path, across the road, and in through a tiny little gate he could only just squeeze through.

There, facing him, was the biggest stable door he had ever seen. He pushed it open, and stood amazed to find himself in quite the most beautiful barn he had ever been in. Even Eeyore felt a strange feeling of quietness and peace.

Eeyore in the Vicar's garden.

In front of him, the path led to a beautiful table.

His little hooves clicked on the stone floor as he moved inside to see more. In front of him the path led to a beautiful table ... there were large silver candles, a big cross, and just below, oh dear, a lovely arrangement of flowers.

Eeyore forgot how lovely and quiet it was, and started to trot towards the flowers. He was feeling a little bit hungry, and still feeling naughty. He had almost reached them when he stopped suddenly.

He could not believe his eyes! There in front of him was a window, and in the window was a picture of *himself*. He moved slowly towards it, not really able to believe what he saw.

Yes, it *was* himself. It was a great big picture, with lots of people in it, all kneeling or standing looking at a little baby who was lying in *his* manger, and there he was, right at the front ... nearer than anyone else to the baby.

He stood looking at it carefully and thoughtfully, then looking round he saw more coloured windows, and he trotted round each of these, looking at them. In the very last one he found what he was looking for and he stood and gave a big, big sigh.

This time, there he was again, with a kind-looking man in a long white gown and many, many people all cheering and waving to him. And *he*, Eeyore, was in the centre of the picture.

Eeyore stood before it, deep in thought. He had seen so many sad,

Yes, it was him, right in front.

ill, beaten and dejected donkeys arriving at the Sanctuary, and his very best friend Ruff had told him of the terrible things that men had done to him before he was rescued.

Could it be that he and his friends had really done something good in the past?

It really did look like it. After all, the very special Man was sitting on *his* back, and not only Eeyore, but all his friends had a cross on their backs like the one on the big table. If this was true, then why did some people ill-treat donkeys so?

Eeyore stood very quietly. Perhaps he had not always been such a naughty donkey, and if he had been so useful before, perhaps he would be chosen to be useful again.

A large tear rolled down Eeyore's cheek.

Suddenly Eeyore felt very ashamed of himself ... Whatever had he run away for and why had he been so unkind to Gertrude? A large tear rolled down his cheek. He took a long last look at the window, remembering every detail to tell the other donkeys, and then, very quietly, on tip-hooves, he left the Church.

Eeyore trotted quickly past the Vicarage, past Mr Green's garden, and up the lane. He broke into a steady canter which he kept up all the way home, and he breathed a sigh of relief to find the gates still open. He felt even luckier when he was able to creep back into his stable unnoticed. He lay down to rest, and to think about what he had seen ...

He heard a voice which seemed to come from a long way away.

"Wake up, Eeyore. It's tea time and you have been asleep all day. I wonder what you have been dreaming about?"

Mother was kneeling beside him, hugging him gently.

"I expect you are sorry that you were so unkind to Gertrude, and you must have been overtired, as you slept all day. Ruff, Pancho and Frosty are coming in for tea now."

Eeyore suddenly felt very happy. Mother still loved him, even though he had been very naughty, and even if his adventures had only been in his dreams, they seemed so real and important that he knew he had to tell the others.

The next day, as soon as he went out to play, he went up to Gertrude, who looked at him with a rather sad expression.

"I really am *so* sorry Gertrude," he said, "and because I was so

"I really am so sorry."

51

They were standing quietly, listening to Eeyore.

unkind to you, you are going to be the very first to know my secret, which I know will make you proud and happy."

He told her all about his day, and how wonderful a part the donkeys had played in the most important event in history.

When he stopped, he looked round, and every other donkey in the Sanctuary was listening. Their eyes were shining, and they were standing quietly, tails swishing gently, a strange proud but sad look on their faces.

"Thank you for telling us, Eeyore," said Lucky Lady, the oldest donkey in the Sanctuary.

"Suddenly I feel that perhaps I have been of some little use in life," and she walked quietly away.

Eeyore knew after what had happened that he would never be an unkind and naughty little donkey again ... well ... not until the next time!

THE STORY OF JACKO
The Hurricane Donkey

Jacko was a very lucky donkey. He was lucky for three reasons.

The first reason was that he lived on a beautiful island called St Lucia in the Caribbean. The village that he lived in was called Gros Islet and it had water on two sides. In front of the village was the sea with a beautiful golden sandy beach and alongside the houses the sea flowed in, like a river, making a large lagoon where the fishermen's boats could anchor safely. On the other two sides of the village, there were large grassy fields which went nearly all the way to the mountains.

The second reason why Jacko was lucky was that he had a very

Jacko was never lonely.

Jacko and Mary had a charming little foal named Donko.

good master called Christoff Bruno. Christoff Bruno was the oldest
brother of nine children and he lived with his mother, brothers and
sisters in a small house on the edge of the village. His father had been
killed while riding his horse, so Christoff Bruno had to work very
hard to help his mother and look after his brothers and sisters.

Christoff Bruno loved Jacko, as did all the children, especially
Gilbert and Smith, two of his younger brothers. Jacko was never
lonely, and loved giving the boys rides in the early morning and
evening when it was cool and he had finished work.

The third reason why Jacko was lucky was that he lived with a
fine donkey mare called Mary and they had a charming little colt foal
that the children had named Donko. Because Christoff Bruno and the
boys were so kind, the donkeys got a great deal of attention. They
were brushed every day and had the stones taken out of their little
hooves, which never grew too long because they wore them down on

When Donko was thirsty, Mary would let him suckle.

the sun-baked earth. They were never hungry because, when they were short of grass at home, Christoff Bruno would lead them into the country to let them graze the sweet, lush grass that grew there.

Because Mary's foal was so little, Christoff Bruno never took her to work, but left her tethered on a very long rope in a small field of grass between the houses and the sea. He would tie one end of the rope to the collar around Mary's neck and the other end to a piece of wood driven deep into the ground.

Whilst Mary grazed quietly, Donko would gallop and play around her and, when he was thirsty, Mary would let him suckle.

Every morning Christoff Bruno got up very early. By the time the sun was rising at six o'clock, he would be untethering Jacko. He always had a careful look at Mary and Donko and, when he was sure they were all right, he would lead Jacko back to the house and tie

56

him up. Carefully, he would put the large wooden pannier on Jacko's back and tie the ropes under his belly. The pannier was padded with palm fronds so that it did not rub Jacko. When it was firmly in place, Christoff Bruno would set off to the country to start his day's work.

Christoff Bruno would spend all day working in the country. Some days he would cut the big stalks of bananas that grew there and then, covering them in sacking, he would load them onto Jacko's back. Jacko would carry them carefully back to the village to be unloaded before he set off again. Sometimes, if Jacko was feeling naughty, he would just manage to twist his head right around and pinch one of the bananas. He would walk along the road with his big load, happily chewing the banana still in its skin!

When Christoff Bruno brought Jacko and his load back to the

Sometimes Jacko would twist his head right round and pinch one of the bananas.

Jacko would enjoy a long, long drink.

village, he always let Jacko have a few moments' rest by the bank while he checked that his mother was all right. He would leave him the family's large white plastic bucket full of cold, clear water, and Jacko would enjoy a long, long drink. By the middle of the day, the temperature was often over eighty degrees and the sun was very strong. Jacko loved the cool breeze that blew in from the sea.

Sometimes, instead of carrying bananas, he would carry cotton sticks and logs to Christoff Bruno's uncle who was a butcher. Every Friday, Jacko had to carry a large load of bananas to the market in Castries which is the capital of St Lucia. Christoff Bruno and Jacko would leave very early in the morning but, however soon they arrived, the market always seemed very busy. Once the bananas were unloaded and sold, Christoff Bruno would buy meat, which Jacko would carry back to the uncle. He would cook the meat in a big pan and sell it. He used the sticks and logs Jacko had carried for his fire, so Jacko was very, very useful to the family and was a very good and obedient donkey.

When Jacko came home on a Friday night, he was always

especially hot and tired and, as a special treat, Christoff Bruno would fetch the big plastic bucket, fill it full of water and slowly pour it over Jacko's head and shoulders. Although donkeys normally hate water, Jacko loved this more than anything. Mary and Donko always loved to watch and, just sometimes, Christoff Bruno would pour some over Mary, but *never* over Donko because little donkeys should never get too wet or they might become ill.

One very hot summer day in August, Jacko began to feel worried. The morning had started as every other morning did and Christoff Bruno was busy working in the banana plantation while Jacko wandered around grazing on the lush grass, which was very much tastier than that at home. Usually Christoff Bruno would load him up just before lunchtime, but this morning was different. It was very, very hot and very, very still, and that was unusual, as there was nearly always a breeze in St Lucia.

Christoff Bruno would fill the bucket full of water and slowly pour it over Jacko's head.

The village looked deserted.

Jacko looked up at the sky and he did not like that either. It was a funny yellow colour and it was gradually getting darker even though it was not even midday. Suddenly he heard Christoff Bruno running towards him and felt the sudden weight of the bananas being put on his back. He gave a small bray of surprise as he felt the sharp sting of a stick on his back, for Christoff Bruno had never ever hit him before.

"Quick, Jacko, we must hurry home! I think a hurricane is coming. We must rescue Mary and Donko because the sea will come right over their field. Then we must make sure that mother and the children board up the windows of the house and that they all hide in there."

Hurricanes are very frightening ... The wind blows as hard as it can, so hard that it can knock over houses and trees that get in its way, and everybody in the Caribbean is afraid when one is coming.

Jacko needed no more telling, and he trotted the mile and a half home as quickly as he could, with Christoff Bruno running in front trying to make him go even faster.

When they reached the village, the sea was already rough and the wind was blowing harder and stronger. Christoff Bruno tied Jacko up with Mary and Donko and ran to help his mother and brothers, who were already banging large boards across the windows. With big, frightened eyes, the donkeys watched the washing on the line blowing harder and harder and the trees bending and swaying as the hurricane came nearer. The village looked deserted; all the people were hiding in their houses.

As the wind blew more strongly, the three donkeys stood shivering together. Jacko and Mary put Donko between them and they turned their backs to the howling wind. Mary gave a snort of fear as she

Christoff Bruno began to run, pulling the donkeys behind him.

realized that the sea was beginning to run into the field. They desperately kept lifting their hooves to keep them out of the swirling water. Donko was really scared, as the water came higher and higher.

The noise was so loud that they did not even hear Christoff Bruno arrive and were surprised to feel halters over their heads as he quickly tied the ropes. They felt a strong tug as Christoff Bruno began to run, pulling the donkeys behind him.

"I must take you to the mountains where you will be safe."

"I must take you up to the mountains where you will be safe," he said. "Your field will soon be flooded and you might all drown."

The donkeys were very frightened and went as fast as they could towards the mountains and safety, behind Christoff Bruno. Donko had a terrible job to keep up.

"Wheeeeee ... whoooooo ... wheeeeee ... whooooooo," went the wind, louder and louder and

The donkeys went as fast as they could behind Christoff Bruno.

louder. It was so loud that they could hardly hear Christoff Bruno
calling, "Faster, faster; the hurricane is coming! You must gallop!"

The three donkeys broke into a gallop to get to safety before the
hurricane hit them.

At last, they reached the mountains, and Christoff Bruno led them
between two large rocks and let them stop to rest. Donko lay down;
he was so tired that he wanted to sleep and sleep and never wake up.
His little hooves hurt and his heart was beating so fast that he could
hardly hear the hurricane.

"Wheeeeee … whoooooo …" went the wind and then down came
the rain. Christoff Bruno covered Donko with his jacket.

It rained so hard that the donkeys could not even see each other.
Jacko and Mary huddled together over Donko, frightened and tired,
as they heard trees crashing down all around them.

The hurricane lasted all night, and it was not until dawn that Christoff Bruno, wet, tired and very worried, led them slowly down the mountain and home.

What a terrible journey it was! Trees had fallen all along the track. Little Donko had a real struggle to jump over some of them, but Christoff Bruno was always there to help. They began to think they would never get home and they wondered what had happened to the family and the village.

At last they got back, and what a sight met their eyes! Cars had been turned over, roofs had been torn off and many of the houses were at strange angles. Christoff Bruno did not even bother to tether the donkeys, but left them and ran to his house calling to his mother, brothers and sisters. What a happy moment when they all appeared

Christoff Bruno covered Donko with his jacket.

They were so happy to
see the donkeys back
safely.

at the windows and door, smiling because they were safe, and they were so happy to see the donkeys back safely.

The three donkeys stood quietly watching, still feeling the wet ground under their little hooves. Jacko looked at their field and saw that the sea actually covered the stake they had been tethered to. He looked at Mary and Donko, both safe and well, and went up to Christoff Bruno and gently nuzzled his hand.

"Thank you," he seemed to say. "Thank you for saving us all," and with tears in his eyes Christoff Bruno bent down and hugged him.

THE CHAMPION DONKEYS

This story is about two donkeys who have been made into champions.

Sam was a strong well built donkey, who lived with loving owners. He had a beautiful paddock, divided into two parts with a stream running down the middle. There was a little bridge over which he could trot to get from one side to the other, and to visit the house where his owner gave him titbits. He shared his paddock with several sheep who ate the grass with him.

Every day Sam spent as much time as he could at the house, before being taken back to his stable for the night, but one day, instead of going back over the bridge, his owner put a nice red head-collar over his head, and took him for a walk down the country lanes, over the big stone road bridge, and into his field. It was over a mile, but Sam loved every minute — he pulled delicious branches out of the

He snatched at succulent grass growing by the roadside.

Sam just refused *to go over the bridge.*

hedgerows and chewed them, and he snatched at succulent grass growing by the roadside. He was sad to be put back in his stable.

The next evening, when his owner tried to take him back over the little wooden bridge, Sam decided that he would rather go round the lanes and he just refused to go over the bridge. He dug his little feet in, and despite pushing, pulling and encouraging — even with his favourite carrots — he just would not go. Finally his owner had to put on his head-collar, and Sam walked proudly back through the lanes.

He was very stubborn, but he loved being stroked and cuddled, because really he was very lonely without another donkey. He knew he should like the sheep, but he decided they were stupid and silly, and one night he did a terribly naughty thing.

He didn't really mean to, but one of the sheep was in *his* stable when he got back from the lane. He chased it out, kicking and biting at it, and then, once he had started, he got naughtier and naughtier, and chased all the others. His owner came running out and was horrified to find the poor sheep in such a state, and the vet was called.

He looked at Sam, who was still feeling cross and angry, and said, "I'm afraid this donkey is unsafe — he will have to go."

Luckily, as soon as Mother heard Sam's problems she said, "Of course, he must come here — with lots of friends I'm sure he will be good."

So the big lorry went to pick him up. Neil, the driver, who is used to getting naughty donkeys into the lorry, had one of his hardest jobs ever, but at last Sam was on his way to the Sanctuary, his owner really sad to see him go.

He just couldn't believe his eyes when he arrived! He didn't know that there were other donkeys in the world, and to meet so many was

Neil had one of his hardest jobs ever.

With Peter and John.

a terrible shock! He was put in a lovely big shelter with nine other donkeys, and suddenly he did not feel quite so important and bossy as before. He wanted to run away and kick when Peter, the Vet, came to give him an injection to protect him from getting ill, but Peter had met naughty donkeys before and Sam didn't have a chance! He soon settled into Sanctuary life, and loved being able to gallop in the large meadows, and having lots of companions once his isolation period was over.

It was a long time before he made a special friend, but one morning he watched from the corner of his eye as Peter and John, the Farm Manager, walked across the field. He was sure they were coming towards him, and had just decided he'd explore the other side of the field when they stopped.

"Joanne says he's very strong and intelligent and would be really good," John was saying. Sam pricked up his ears — were they really talking about him?

The isolation block.

"Let's give him a try then," said Peter the Vet. "Mother thinks he's a lovely donkey."

Before Sam had time really to think about it, John slipped a head-collar over his head, and, full of curiosity, Sam went happily with them back to the main yard of the Sanctuary.

Standing there was another donkey, very like himself. He was called Dobby.

Dobby had had a lonely life as well. For the last twelve years he had been running wild on a farm with cows and his feet had grown longer and longer, until someone had complained to the R.S.P.C.A., who keep an eye on all animals. They had called the Donkey Sanctuary, who had persuaded the owner to let Dobby come to Devon, where he could be loved and cared for. Dobby had been with Mother for two years, and, with special care, his feet were now perfect, and he was a happy, contented donkey.

He and Sam nuzzled each other and, after a little pushing and shoving, just to prove who was boss, Sam decided he was perhaps just a little bit better than Dobby, but he thought that Dobby would make a fine friend.

For a week they got to know each other, living in a special paddock with their own private stable. Each night they wondered why they were so special and, I'm afraid, began to get a little bit bored.

Sam was too fat — perhaps because of all the titbits he had so lovingly received, and the fact that he had eaten far more of the grass than the sheep had. Now fat donkeys are not fit donkeys, so Peter had put him on a diet, so that he could lose a little weight. On this particular night he felt really hungry!

"Come on," he said to Dobby, "if we work it out, I'm sure we can open the gate together."

The naughty donkeys spent ages pushing and pulling, until at last Dobby got his head under the bars and lifted the gate. Sam got his little teeth round the bolt and pulled! Suddenly the gate was open!

Actually, they were rather surprised that they had managed it. For a few moments they stood quietly, to see if anyone had heard, then both together, they began to explore. Normally Joanne left bales of hay just outside their stable, but by chance she had used the last one that night!

Sam led the way on to the main drive and up towards the road. They were disappointed to find a big red rail blocking their way, and when they tried to go under it, their little hooves got stuck in the cattle grid.

They soon gave up trying that way of escape, and trotted back down the drive, past the Information Room. There in front of their eyes was the hay barn. With a bray of delight, Sam dived in! But the bray was his undoing. Neil, on night duty, was just returning from his rounds, and instinct told him that this was a naughty bray coming from the wrong place!

Whilst Dobby nuzzled him, loving company, Neil and Sam glared at each other. Sam's mouth was full of hay!

"I might have guessed it was you," said Neil, recognizing him at once and remembering their last experience. "Come on, you're

Their little feet got stuck in the cattle grid.

supposed to be on a diet!!" and he led them back to their stable, not without some difficulty.

Neil put them in and pretended to walk away, but hid behind the stable. As soon as Sam thought Neil had gone, he encouraged Dobby to help him with the gate again!

"Oh no you don't, my son," said Neil, as soon as he saw what they were doing, and with baler twine he firmly fastened the gate!

The next morning Mother came, and tried to be cross with them, but they looked so sorry she forgave them, and told them something very special would soon be happening. Very shortly they got their first clue! John and Joanne arrived with Tracey, who had been working in the Slade Centre, where donkeys give rides to handicapped children.

They were taken out to one of the big fields where Mother was waiting.

"You are very important donkeys," said Mother. "You have been chosen out of all donkeys here to see if you can be taught how to

76

plough, because the Donkey Sanctuary has been asked to give a display at the National Ploughing Championships, and you have the chance to show the people in England what donkeys can do, and *are* doing abroad."

Talking to Mother.

Sam and Dobby felt *very* proud. "You have been chosen because you are strong, fit and intelligent," Mother went on, "and I hope you won't let us down."

Sam and Dobby were sure they had grown two feet taller, and were determined to do their best, but, oh dear …

And then their training started!

Joanne and Tracey fastened the long reins on them, and side by side they set off across the fields.

Longreining.

"Whoopee," said Sam, and broke into a gallop! Dobby joined in, and the peaceful scene was changed in a second! The geriatric donkeys, that is, all the donkeys over thirty-five years old, lifted their heads in amazement, slowly chewing the grass in their mouths, their eyes opening wider and wider, as poor Joanne and Tracey were dragged across the field! However, after a week, Dobby and Sam had worked out how to do it, and felt very satisfied with themselves.

The next step was to pull one of the little traps the Slade Centre children used. This was fine until Sam walked across the metal cover of a drain in the road — the clatter of his little hooves was enough for him, and, dragging a reluctant Dobby, he set off at a gallop up the road, the cart careering behind them, with Tracey hanging on! He was naughty!

After a week, it was Dobby who was in trouble. He wanted to stop and talk to everybody: one minute the cart would be flying up

Peter examining after the ploughing.

the road, and the next it stopped dead, if Dobby saw a friend! But gradually things began to improve, and car owners began to get used to meeting a little trap drawn by two donkeys in the Devon lanes.

Finally, Sam and Dobby were introduced to the plough! In many parts of the world, donkeys have to plough, as their owners do not have tractors, so the Sanctuary had  helped by designing a suitable plough for them, and Sam and Dobby were harnessed up to this. What a fuss was made of them! Special bandages were put round their legs, with flaps to make sure the chains could not rub them. The donkeys loved the fuss and attention!

The first day, John went behind the plough to steer it, with Joanne and Tracey leading the donkeys. At first they found it hard, but once they learnt to pull together it got easier, and after ploughing three long furrows, Peter the Vet examined them. Sam was pleased to hear him say how well they both were.

They practised and practised until they were perfect!

At long last it was the day of the big show! They arrived early and watched with amazement as the most  *enormous* horses came out of the arriving trucks. The donkeys began to feel very small indeed! They were known as shire horses. Years ago some had been used to pull big carts round the city streets, but most had been owned by farmers and spent their lives ploughing. It was a job horses knew they could do, and they looked very surprised to see the donkeys there; some of their handlers even laughed at Sam and Dobby.

Crowds and crowds of people arrived and the donkeys were given a small field to plough. All around them the horses were working, and they could hear calls of, "Come on there, Rosy — get on, Neddy."

John was really smartly dressed, and wore a nice red tie. Joanne

and Tracey had red ribbons in their pony tails to match the donkeys' smart leggings and brow bands.

They started to plough. At first no-one seemed to notice them, but gradually more and more people arrived, and as they reached the last furrow everybody started clapping!

Sam and Dobby nearly burst with pride — they had worked together, all naughty thoughts gone from their heads, and they had really shown what donkeys could do.

When they had finished, John, Joanne and Tracey unharnessed them and seemed really happy, and they were sure Mother had tears in her eyes as she gave them a cuddle and congratulated them all.

I'm not surprised they won a big trophy for the best Donkey Ploughing Team — are you?